For Daniel Winterbottom–J.G.

For Nancy Lawton–N.R.

Gamma Productions offers a wide variety
of books for children of all ages. For
information on ordering, please write:

Gamma Productions, Inc.
1490 Route 23
Wayne N.J. 07470

Published by Goodmaster Books,
a division of Gamma Productions
ISBN 0-937235-04-0
Originally published by Parents Magazine Press
ISBN 0-8193-1015-8

Willy's Raiders

Story by
JACK GANTOS

Art by
NICOLE RUBEL

Goodmaster Books • New York

Willy Raccoon was the captain of his
baseball team. They were called
Willy's Raiders because Willy was
the best player. He could hit,
he could catch, and he could pitch.
He liked stealing bases, too.

Willy and his team members were all
good sports. They practiced hard
and were the best team in the league.
The Raiders were very proud
of themselves because they always
played fair and square.

After winning, they always
shook hands with the losers.
And even if they lost a game,
which sometimes happened,
they never complained.

But there was one team that did not
play fair and square—the Weasels.
All day long they sat around their
clubhouse saying nasty things
about all the other teams.
They were too lazy to practice
and had to win by cheating.

Once the Weasels beat the Beavers
by hiding the bases from them.
Each time a Beaver hit the ball,
he could never find first base
and was soon tagged out.

"You guys are stupid!" the Weasels said
to the Beavers after the game was over.
Then they laughed all the way back
to their clubhouse.
The Beavers were angry but couldn't
do a thing about it.

Another time the Weasels beat the Rabbits
by sneakily coating their bats with grease.
Each time a Rabbit took a swing,
his bat flew through the air.

"You Rabbits should learn how to
play this game," snickered the Weasels.
"It's the ball that's supposed to fly
through the air."

The Rabbits were very upset.
But there was nothing they could do
since the Weasels were so mean and nasty.

The only team the Weasels
could not beat was Willy's Raiders.
No matter how much the Weasels cheated,
they could not win. Willy was just
too smart and too good for them.

He always avoided their dirty tricks
and led his team to victory.
This made the Weasels very mad
because they wanted to win
the championship.

Still, at the end of the season,
the Raiders and Weasels were tied
for first place.

"The championship game is tomorrow,"
said Captain Sneaky Weasel to his team.
"And we have to beat those Raiders!"

"But how?" asked Creepo Weasel.
"With Willy on their team we can
never win."

"We have to get Willy out of the way,"
said Nasty Weasel.
"That's right," agreed Lazy Weasel.

"I've got a sneaky fail-proof plan,"
replied the captain.
"Follow me and we'll make sure
Willy doesn't play tomorrow!"

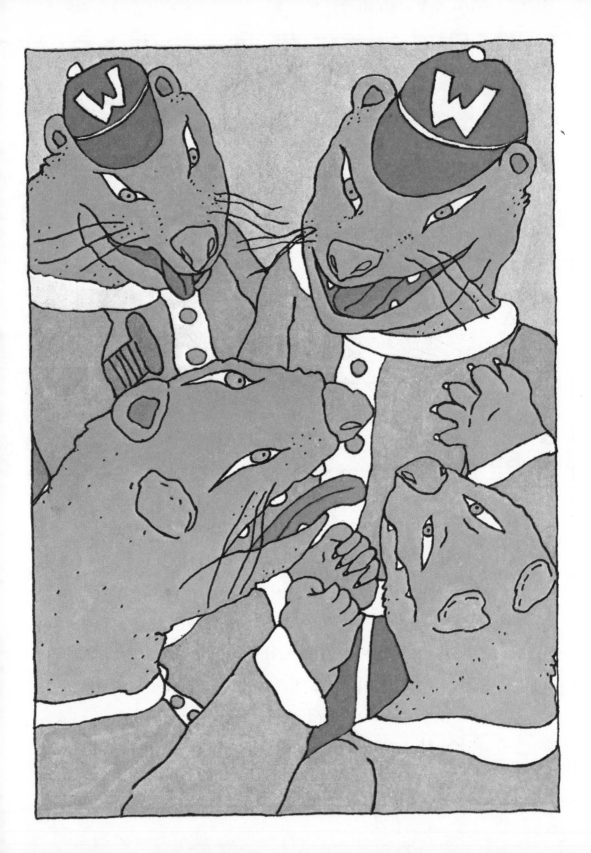

The morning of the championship game
Willy woke up bright and early.
He was putting on his uniform
when he smelled something good
cooking outside his window.
"Red-hot hot dogs for sale!" cried
a sneaky voice behind a hot-dog stand.
"Fresh popcorn, candy apples, root beer!"

"I should get something to eat before
the game starts," Willy thought to himself.
"After all, I have to be in top shape
in order to beat those Weasels."
So he went outside.

"I'll take two of everything,"
said Willy as he sat down.
But before Willy could finish eating,
the Weasels sneaked up on him
behind his back.

"We've got you now!" they shouted as
they dropped a trash can over his head.

Before Willy knew what happened,
he was trapped.
"Help!" he cried out. "Help! Help!"
But there was no one around
to save him.

The Weasels tied down the top of
the trash can. Then they pushed it
up a hill to hide Willy from his team.
"You'll never get away with this!"
cried Willy.
"Baloney!" replied Sneaky Weasel.
"Without you, the Raiders are sure to lose."

Soon they reached the top of the hill.
"We'll let you out after we win
the championship," snickered the Weasels.
Willy could hear them laughing
as they ran back down the hill
towards the baseball field.

When Willy didn't show up for the game
on time, his teammates were upset.
"This isn't at all like Willy,"
said Rhonda Raccoon.
"He's always on time," said Henry Raccoon.

"I bet those Weasels have something
to do with it," said Bruno Raccoon.
"They never play fair and square."
Just then the Weasels arrived.
They all had big nasty grins on their faces.

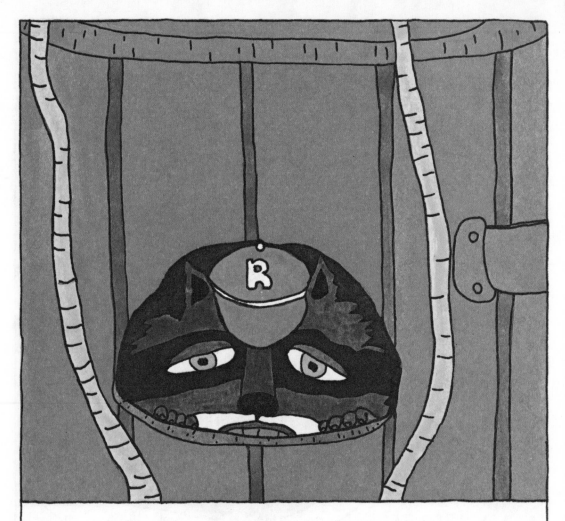

Soon the game began.
Through a hole in the trash can
Willy could look down the hill
and watch his team.
Without him, the Raiders were losing.

Willy could see the Weasels
moving the bases around
and greasing the Raiders' bats.
They even rode their
bicycles around the bases.
And to top it all off,
Captain Sneaky Weasel was
throwing unfair spitballs.

Willy was furious. "I can't
take this any longer!" he shouted.
"Those creepy Weasels have gone too far!"
He beat on the sides with his fists.
He stood on his head and kicked the lid.
After that, he flopped around

like a Mexican jumping bean . . .
until suddenly the trash can fell over.
"Oh, no!" cried Willy as it rolled down the hill.
"Somebody get me out of here!"
But the can kept going faster and faster,
rolling and bumping down the hill.

It rolled onto the playing field
and rolled over Captain Sneaky Weasel.
Finally it stopped in the Raiders' dugout.
"Get me out of here!" shouted Willy.
Henry and Rhonda Raccoon quickly
untied the lid and Willy crawled out.

"What do we do next, Captain?"
asked Bruno when Willy was no longer dizzy.
"Let's show those nasty Weasels
who has the best team," cried Willy.
"Hooray!" shouted the Raiders.

When Willy came out on the field,
the Weasels were upset.
"Boo!" they shouted. "Boo! Hiss!"
But that didn't bother Willy.

He hit home runs. He stole bases.
And his pitching was so fast that
he struck out the Weasels all in a row.
Soon the game was over and the Raiders
had won.

When Willy and the Raiders picked up
their championship trophy, the Weasels
all had frowns on their faces.
"We'll get you next season!" cried
Captain Sneaky Weasel as he limped away.
"No, you won't," replied Willy.
"Because the good guys always win."

Then the Raiders put Willy on
their shoulders and went back to
their clubhouse to celebrate.

ABOUT THE AUTHOR AND ARTIST

JACK GANTOS and NICOLE RUBEL met at a
costume party. He came as a giant rabbit.
She came as Alice (from Wonderland). They
have gone on to create memorable picture
book characters together, including Rotten
Ralph. And true to the spirit in which they
met, during the school year they travel to
classrooms dressed as their characters and
act out their books.

JACK GANTOS has lived in a variety of
places, including Florida and several Carib-
bean islands. Now he calls Boston home.
In addition to his own writing, he teaches
writing at Emerson College there.

NICOLE RUBEL, who grew up as a twin in
Florida, also makes her home in Boston.
She spends her working time in her studio,
illustrating books and painting. Last year,
her first painting show was put on display.